-HAUNTED HISTORY-

EDINBURGH CASTLE IS HAUNTED!

MARIE MORRISON

PowerKiDS press.

NEW YORK

Published in 2021 by The Rosen Publishing Group, Inc.
29 East 21st Street, New York, NY 10010

Editor: Jill Keppeler
Book Design: Rachel Rising

Portions of this work were originally authored by Ryan Nagelhout and published as *Haunted! Edinburgh Castle.* All new material this edition authored by Marie Morrison.

Photo Credits: Cover, JoannaTkaczuk/Shutterstock.com; pp. 1–32 (background) Slava Gerj/Shutterstock.com; pp. 5, 9 Colin Dewar/Shutterstock.com; p. 7 bonoc/Shutterstock.com; p. 11 Zsolt Nagy/Shutterstock.com; p. 13 anastas_styles/Shutterstock.com; p. 15 Culture Club/ Hulton Archive/Getty Images; p. 16 anastas_styles/Shutterstock.com; pp. 17, 23 David Cheskin - PA Images/ PA Images/ Getty Images; p. 18 Iordanis/Shutterstock.com; p. 19 JeniFoto/Shutterstock.com; p. 21 Claudio Divizia/Shutterstock.com; pp. 25, 29 Jeff J Mitchell/Staff/Getty Images; p. 26 CI Photos/Shutterstock.com; p. 27 Anna Kucherova/Shutterstock.com; p. 30 jan kranendonk/Shutterstock.com.

Cataloging-in-Publication Data

Names: Morrison, Marie.
Title: Edinburgh Castle is haunted! / Marie Morrison.
Description: New York : PowerKids Press, 2021. | Series: Haunted history | Includes glossary and index.
Identifiers: ISBN 9781725319929 (pbk.) | ISBN 9781725319943 (library bound) | ISBN 9781725319936 (6 pack)
Subjects: LCSH: Edinburgh Castle (Edinburgh, Scotland)--Juvenile literature. | Haunted castles--Scotland--Juvenile literature. | Ghosts--Scotland--Edinburgh--Juvenile literature.
Classification: LCC F1474.M67 2021 | DDC 133.1'294134--dc23

Manufactured in the United States of America

Some of the images in this book illustrate individuals who are models. The depictions do not imply actual situations or events.

CPSIA Compliance Information: Batch #CSPK20. For further information contact Rosen Publishing, New York, New York at 1-800-237-9932.

CONTENTS

A SCOTTISH STRONGHOLD

For at least 3,000 years, humans have gathered at Castle Rock in Edinburgh, Scotland. This volcanic peak has been home to residents from ancient Celts right up to Scottish royalty. Today, Edinburgh Castle still stands on its perch, keeping watch over the city below.

Historians say that Castle Rock and Edinburgh Castle are some of the most attacked and besieged sites in Europe—so it's probably no surprise that the castle has many legends and ghost stories. There are tales of ghostly inhabitants that include accused witches, lost pipers, and even a mourning dog. Its ancient buildings and mysterious rooms and tunnels have captured the imaginations of many. Read on, and see if you agree that Edinburgh Castle is haunted!

Castle Rock, on which Edinburgh Castle stands, formed about 340 million years ago.

BEFORE THE CASTLE

One of the first settlements on Castle Rock was Din Eidyn, or "Fort Eidyn." The Votadini (or Gododdin), a British tribe, built the fort there sometime before AD 600, although there's evidence people lived there even longer ago than that, back into the Iron or even Bronze Ages. A map dating back to the second century BC marks the site as Alauna, or "rock place."

By AD 638, the Angles, people from the area now called Germany, captured the area. Din Eidyn became known as Edinburgh. The city grew up around the hilltop fort. However, there's not much further information about the site or the town until the 11th or 12th centuries. No structures from before then remain today.

EDINBURGH CASTLE ISN'T THE OLDEST STANDING CASTLE IN SCOTLAND. THAT HONOR BELONGS TO CASTLE SWEEN IN ARGYLL, SHOWN HERE. AN IRISH CHIEFTAIN PROBABLY BUILT IT IN THE 1100S.

-Stone and Bronze and Iron-

The Stone, Bronze, and Iron Ages are periods of human development in prehistory. The Stone Age started about 3.3 million years ago. The time periods for the Bronze and Iron Ages vary depending on the location, but the Bronze Age (in which people started using metal for tools) started in Scotland about 1900 BC. The Iron Age (in which people started using iron for tools) started about 800 BC.

THE OLDEST BUILDING

The first king who definitely lived on Castle Rock was Malcolm III Canmore, who ruled from 1058 to 1093. However, his wife, Queen Margaret, may be even better remembered there. Starting in 1130, her son, King David I, started building some of the castle structures that remain today. He **dedicated** the chapel to his mother. That building, constructed between 1130 and 1140, is now the oldest surviving part of the castle. In fact, it's the oldest surviving structure in Edinburgh!

Weddings and other ceremonies still take place inside the tiny chapel today. Its basic structure and fancy arches are much the same as they were years ago, although the colorful stained glass windows date from the 20th century. A group makes sure there's always fresh flowers inside the chapel.

Saint Margaret's Chapel is at the highest point of Castle Rock.

Spooky Stuff

Malcolm III Canmore was the son of King Duncan I the ruler famously killed by Macbeth in William Shakespeare's play. Malcolm went on to kill the historical Macbeth in 1057.

GROWING AND CHANGING

Bit by bit, Edinburgh Castle grew. This was **complicated**, though, by how often the Scots and the English fought over it. During the late 13th century into the 14th century, the English captured the castle twice. In 1315, Robert the Bruce, king of Scotland, ordered his men to destroy the castle so the enemy couldn't take it again—and they did, wrecking all but Saint Margaret's Chapel.

The Scots rebuilt the castle in the mid-1300s. The new structure included David's Tower, named in honor of David II, the king at the time. The tower stood for about 200 years before it was destroyed in another siege. By this time, the Great Hall (finished in 1511) and the Royal Palace also stood on Castle Rock as part of the castle.

THE GREAT HALL (SHOWN) AND ROYAL PALACE OF EDINBURGH CASTLE STILL STAND TODAY.

Spooky Stuff

Around the time James VI was born, Scottish royalty started living more in other castles and palaces. The last member of royalty to stay in Edinburgh Castle was Charles I in 1633.

- King James VI -

In 1566, Mary Queen of Scots gave birth at the Royal Palace to her son, James. This son would become King James VI of Scotland in 1567 and King James I of England in 1603. The tiny room where he was born is still a tourist destination today. One of the creepier secrets of the castle lies far below that room, however—a pit that may have been used as a prison!

DUNGEONS AND DUNG

Like any decent castle with a history of hauntings, Edinburgh Castle has dungeons. Captors often tortured the prisoners there. At times, they wouldn't allow prisoners to sleep. Sometimes they used devices such as thumbscrews—which crushed prisoners' thumbs in an agonizing way.

Stories say, of course, that the prisoners from the castle's dungeons may still haunt them. One tale tells of a prisoner who tried to escape by hiding in a wheelbarrow full of **dung**. He did make it out of the dungeon—but he died when the worker pushing the wheelbarrow emptied it over the side of Castle Rock. Today, people say he still haunts the castle, trying to push people off the cliffs and giving away his presence by a bad smell.

SPOOKY STUFF

THE LAST RECORDED TORTURE VICTIM IN EDINBURGH WAS ENGLISH WRITER HENRY NEVILLE PAYNE. HE WAS A PRISONER FOR 10 YEARS AROUND 1690.

Some visitors say they've seen or heard the former prisoners of the Edinburgh Castle dungeons even today.

THE HEAD OF THE BLACK BULL

The ghosts of the young Earl of Douglas and his little brother may not walk the halls of Edinburgh Castle—but no one would blame them if they did! In November 1440, the sixth Earl of Douglas, age 16, and his brother David arrived at the castle for dinner with King James II of Scotland, who was only 10 years old himself.

At the end of the meal, however, there was no dessert. Instead, the visitors were presented with the head of a black bull—a sign of death. Two of the king's advisers had decided the Douglas clan was a threat to the throne. The advisers tried the earl and his brother for treason. They were killed right in front of the young king.

SPOOKY STUFF

The events surrounding the death of the Earl of Douglas and his brother are often called the Black Dinner.

James II was only 6 years old when he became king. Three families fought to control him, but he later became a strong ruler in his own right.

BELOW THE SQUARE

Crown Square has been the main courtyard of the castle since the 15th century. Royal residences, started by members of the Stewart **dynasty**, once surrounded this large open space. The Royal Palace lies to the east, while the Queen Anne building is to the west, the Great Hall lies to the south, and the National War Memorial stands to the north.

Crown Square sits over a naturally uneven part of Castle Rock. King James III had builders construct a series of 120 stone vaults that form the square's foundation. Over the years, these vaults and tunnels held many prisoners of war, who were crammed into these dark, close places while royalty lived above. It's easy to imagine how some of those prisoners might want to haunt the place today!

This photo shows part of a recreation of the prisons in the Crown Square vaults.

-American Graffiti-

Prisoners from all over the world lived in the vaults under Crown Square. There were pirates and sailors. There were prisoners from Denmark, France, Ireland, Italy, Poland, and Spain. During a certain period of time, a number of the prisoners were American sailors captured during the American Revolutionary War. In fact, if you visit the vaults today, you can still see a version of the U.S. flag an early patriot scratched into a door!

LOCH AND KEY

King James II's son, James III, followed his father as king of Scotland in 1460. In 1460, he ordered that a marsh below the castle be flooded to help Edinburgh Castle's defenses, creating a loch, or lake, called the Nor' Loch.

The lake might have been a beautiful place at one point, but it soon developed rather unpleasant connections. Scottish authorities accused many women of witchcraft from the 1500s to the late 1600s. One way of testing an **alleged** witch was to tie her thumbs and toes together and dunk her in the water to see if she drowned. The loch provided a handy place for this. In time, between the number of dead bodies and the waste that residents threw into the loch, it became a stinking pit in the middle of the city.

TODAY, THE SITE OF THE NOR' LOCH IS PART OF THE PRINCES STREET GARDENS.

-SEEING THINGS-

Stories say that the Nor' Loch became so polluted by **sewage** and other things that the **methane** gas and the smell it gave off became so bad that people living nearby began to get sick and to have hallucinations, or see things that weren't there. Many people killed themselves at the site, as well. The city of Edinburgh eventually drained the Nor' Loch.

Witches' Well

If one of the women accused of witchcraft survived her dunking in the Nor' Loch or elsewhere, her accusers would say that meant she was guilty. The accused witch would be burned at the stake, often right at Edinburgh Castle. Today, a fountain called the Witches' Well marks the area and the lives (and deaths) of these women.

One of Edinburgh's most famous prisoners (and perhaps, one of its most famous ghosts) was an accused witch. In 1537, King James V of Scotland accused Janet Douglas, Lady Glamis, of witchcraft and plotting to kill him. He had her burned at the stake. Today, some people say you can hear knocking noises at that part of Edinburgh Castle, the sound of workers building the platform where Janet Douglas died.

Spooky Stuff

James V had servants and friends of Janet Douglas's family tortured to get "confessions" of witchcraft out of them. He even tortured her son, John, who was then forced to watch his mother's death.

More than 300 women were burned at the site of the Witches' Well. Throughout Scotland, more than 4,000 people (mostly women) died during the time of the witch trials.

THE HAUNTED GRAVEYARD

Edinburgh's haunting tales may be centered on the castle, but some of the city's most legendary stories take place not far away. Greyfriars Kirkyard, a **cemetery** in the city's center, dates from the mid-1560s. Its rumored hauntings include George MacKenzie, a famously **ruthless** lawyer who was responsible for the torture and deaths of more than 18,000 people for their faith in the 1600s. So many people died in this struggle over religion that this time period has been called "the Killing Time."

After "Bloody MacKenzie" died in 1691, he was buried in a **mausoleum** in the cemetery—very near the terrible prison where he sent so many people. Visitors often report being scratched, bruised, burned, or otherwise attacked nearby, either by MacKenzie's **poltergeist** or the ghosts of his victims.

In more recent times, a number of people have broken into the MacKenzie mausoleum. Today, the door is kept locked—perhaps to keep people out, or perhaps to keep something in!

SPOOKY STUFF

Some of the graves in Greyfriars Kirkyard (and elsewhere in Edinburgh) have mortsafes, iron cages or stone boxes that enclose them. This was to prevent people from stealing the bodies!

-Greyfriars Bobby-

Greyfriars Kirkyard is also home to a sweeter story. As the story goes, Greyfriars Bobby was a Skye terrier who belonged to a man named John Gray. When Gray died in 1858, he was buried in the cemetery. For 14 years afterward, legends say, Bobby only left the grave to eat. Today, he's buried there near his master. A statue of the dog stands nearby.

THE PIPER IN THE PASSAGES

Another famous Edinburgh Castle ghost story has nothing to do with the old stone buildings rising high over the city or the vaults below, but old tunnels leading away from the castle, down the Royal Mile, deep underground. These tunnels seemed to go toward Holyroodhouse, a royal residence in the city. While many sources aren't quite clear on when the tunnels were discovered, stories say that the discoverers sent a young bagpiper into them to explore.

The idea was that listeners could track the piper by the sound of his playing. However (the stories say), about halfway along the way, the music suddenly stopped. The piper was never seen again, although residents of and visitors to Edinburgh sometimes claim to hear ghostly pipes from underground.

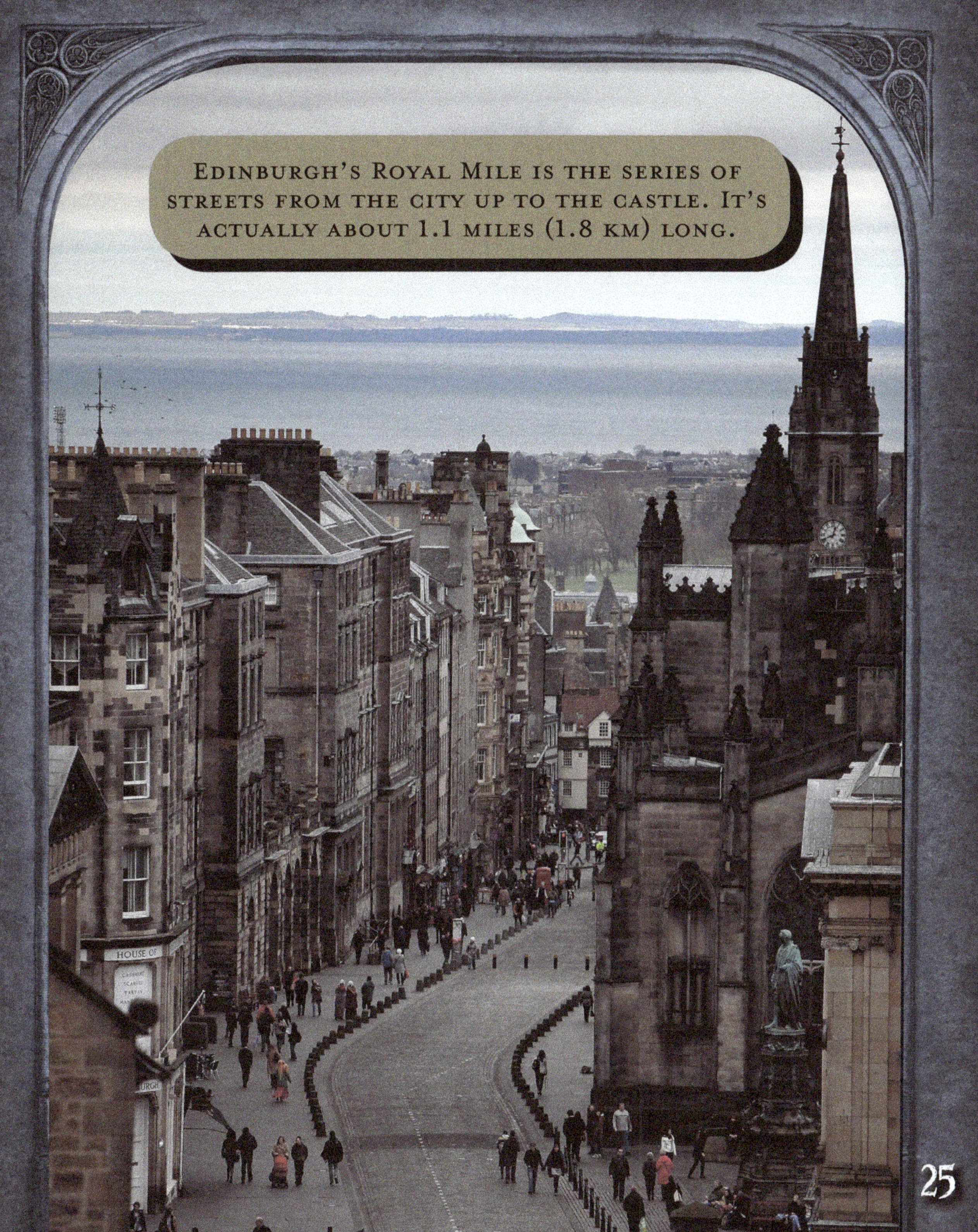

Edinburgh's Royal Mile is the series of streets from the city up to the castle. It's actually about 1.1 miles (1.8 km) long.

A GHOSTLY WARNING SYSTEM

The piper in the passages isn't Edinburgh Castle's only musical ghost. Legend also tells of a headless drummer boy who only appears when the castle is about to come under attack—although people have reported hearing his drum at other times.

The stories say that this ghost first appeared in 1650 when English statesman Oliver Cromwell attacked the castle. The last threat to the castle was back in 1745, when soldiers attacked during the second **Jacobite** uprising. Charles Edward Stuart (also known as Bonnie Prince Charlie) and his army took part of the city but failed to take the castle. Stuart's army (and his rebellion) would be destroyed at Culloden in 1746. Fortunately, no one has seen the headless drummer since.

Can you imagine walking in Edinburgh Castle and hearing the steady beat of a drum—but not being able to see the drummer? Spooky!

SCIENCE AND SPIRITS

Ghosts and real scientific investigation don't seem to mix, but people have tried. In 2001, scientist Dr. Richard Wiseman ran a 10-day investigation of Edinburgh Castle as part of the Edinburgh International Science Festival. He and his researchers used recording equipment and volunteers to seek proof of ghosts in and around the castle.

Although the 240 volunteers didn't know which areas under the castle were already thought to be haunted, Wiseman found that more than half of them reported odd experiences in those areas, while only about a third reported that feeling in other places. Some volunteers said they felt drops in temperature or saw odd shapes. Some felt like they were being watched. Wiseman, who is **skeptical** about ghost stories, noted that the most "haunted" areas were bigger and had darker hallways outside them.

WISEMAN SAID THAT PERHAPS THE SENSE OF NOT KNOWING WHAT WAS GOING ON IN THE HALLWAYS OUTSIDE THE "HAUNTED" AREAS MADE PEOPLE NERVOUS.

VISITING THE CASTLE

You can still visit Edinburgh Castle on Castle Rock today. You can walk through its imposing main gates. You can watch and speak to costumed performers bringing the castle's history to life, or you can take part in tours that show you many of its wonders. You can visit the crown jewels of Scotland, peek into the vaults that once held prisoners, and touch the ancient stones that make up Saint Margaret's Chapel.

Whether or not ghosts haunt the castle, the past is still alive there in its own way. Throughout dozens of battles over the years, Edinburgh Castle has endured and outlasted its attackers. It still watches over Edinburgh today. That's pretty impressive with or without ghosts!

GLOSSARY

alleged: Assert to be true or exist.

cemetery: A place where the dead are buried.

complicate: To make something more difficult.

dedicate: To decide that something will be used for a special purpose or in memory of someone.

dung: Solid waste from an animal.

dynasty: A family that rules over a country for a long time.

Jacobite: Someone who followed James II of England or the Stuart family after 1688.

mausoleum: A stone building where dead bodies are kept.

methane: A colorless gas.

poltergeist: A ghost that makes odd noises and makes things move.

ruthless: Cruel, having no pity or mercy.

sewage: Human waste carried away from homes and other buildings.

skeptical: Expressing doubt about something.

INDEX

WEBSITES

Due to the changing nature of Internet links, PowerKids Press has developed an online list of websites related to the subject of this book. This site is updated regularly. Please use this link to access the list: www.powerkidslinks.com/haunted/edinburgh